Ourselves

KU-113-135

Schools Library and Information Services

S00000643042

My baby sister's head is bare,
She hasn't yet a single hair,
So I've thought of each and every style
That might suit her and make her smile!

Perhaps she'll look like cousin Kate
With funky dreadlocks, they'd be great!
She could wear them long and dangly,
With silver stars to make them spangly!

Baby Kai

Big sister's hair is shocking pink,
A little outrageous, don't you think?
Baby could add streaks to hers,
Or even spots, if she prefers!

Lots of pigtails tied with bows
Would make her look like Auntie Rose.
She could use rainbow elastic,
Now wouldn't that be just fantastic!

Perhaps she'll grow up just like Mum,
And wear her hair up in a bun,
With curls and swirls all over the place
So high they reach to outer space.

But hey! What's Baby hiding there?
Don't tell me she has some hair!
Look at our smiley little girl
With her first and very own real...